Isabelle Harper

MY DOG ROSIE

Illustrated by Barry Moser

SCHOLASTIC INC.

New York   Toronto   London   Auckland   Sydney

Rosie, Izzy, and Barry wish to thank Alexandra Day and the folks at Farrar, Straus
& Giroux for granting permission to print the jacket of *Carl Goes Shopping*
by Alexandra Day—Rosie's favorite book, of course! Copyright © 1989 by
Alexandra Day, used by permission of Farrar, Straus & Giroux, Inc.
Special thanks also to Friskies Pet Care, a division of Nestlé/Carnation
Food Company, for the use of their cat food in this book.
Friskies is a registered trademark of Nestlé Inc.

ISBN 0-590-69863-X

12 11 10 9 8 7 6 5 4 3 2 1   6 7 8 9/9 0 1/0

Printed in the United States of America   08

The illustrations in this book were executed with watercolor on paper
handmade by Simon Green at the Barcham Green Mills in Maidstone, Kent,
Great Britain, especially for the Royal Watercolor Society.
Original Blue Sky Press edition designed by Barry Moser

For Carl

WHEN GRANDPA goes into his room to work,

it's my job to take care of Rosie.

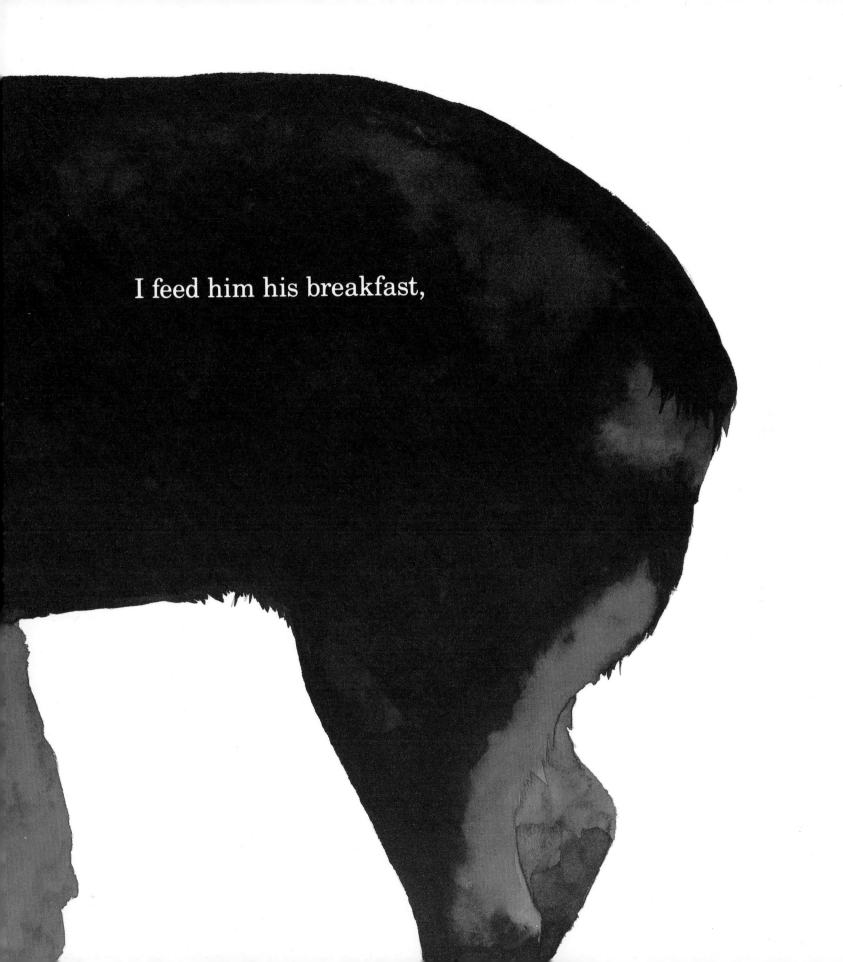

I feed him his breakfast,

I give him his bath,

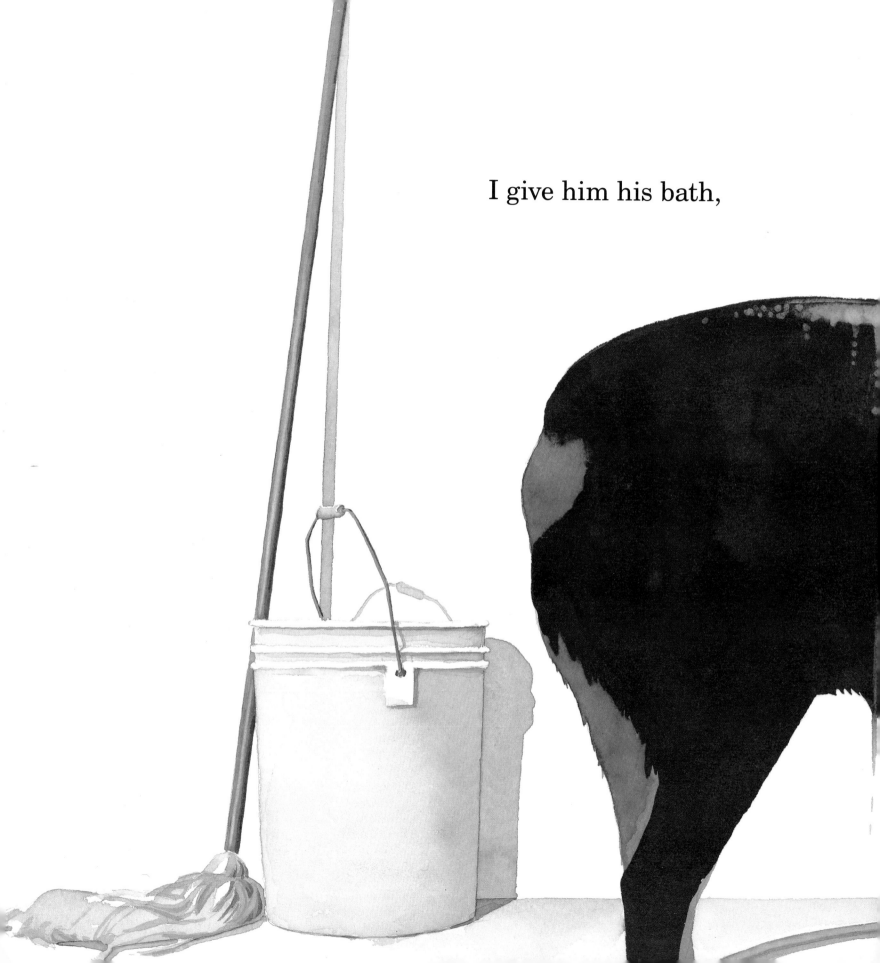

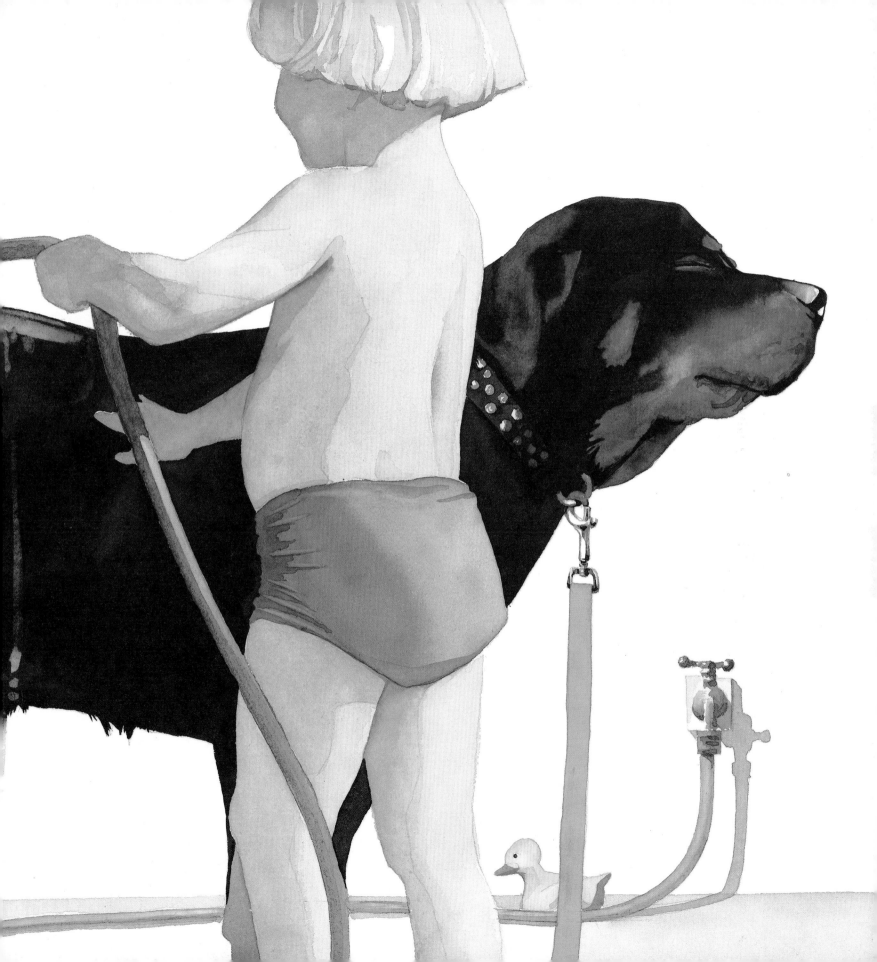

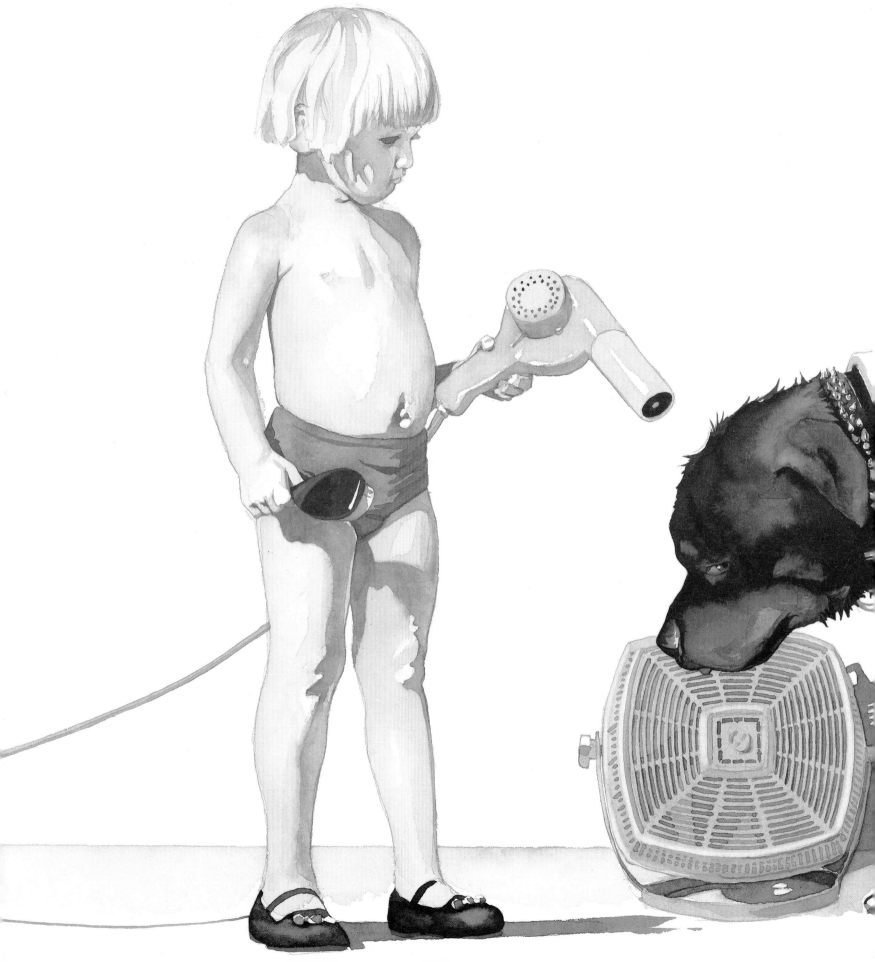

and then I help him dry off before I brush his hair.

I read him his favorite story,

and after that, I take him outside to play.

I throw the ball,

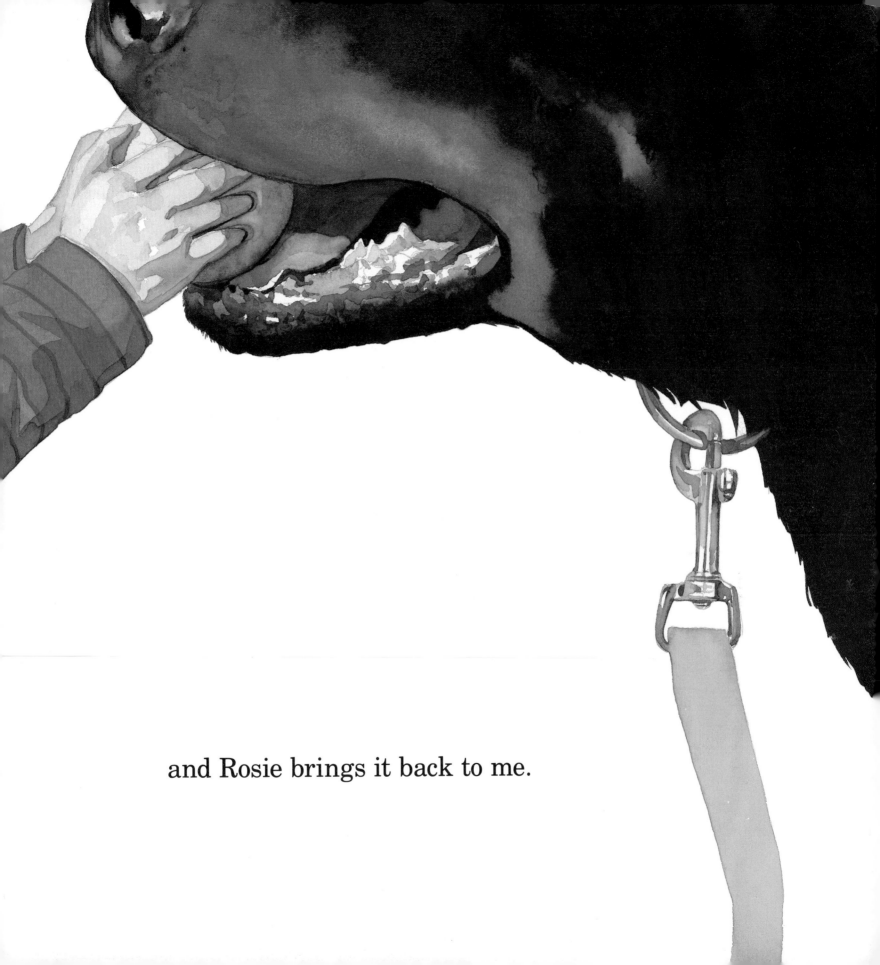

and Rosie brings it back to me.

Woodrow comes along, and he plays with us, too.

Rosie loses the ball.

Woodrow finds it and keeps it.

Rosie is tired. It's time for his nap.

Grandpa helps me with Rosie's quilt.

Soon Rosie is sound asleep.

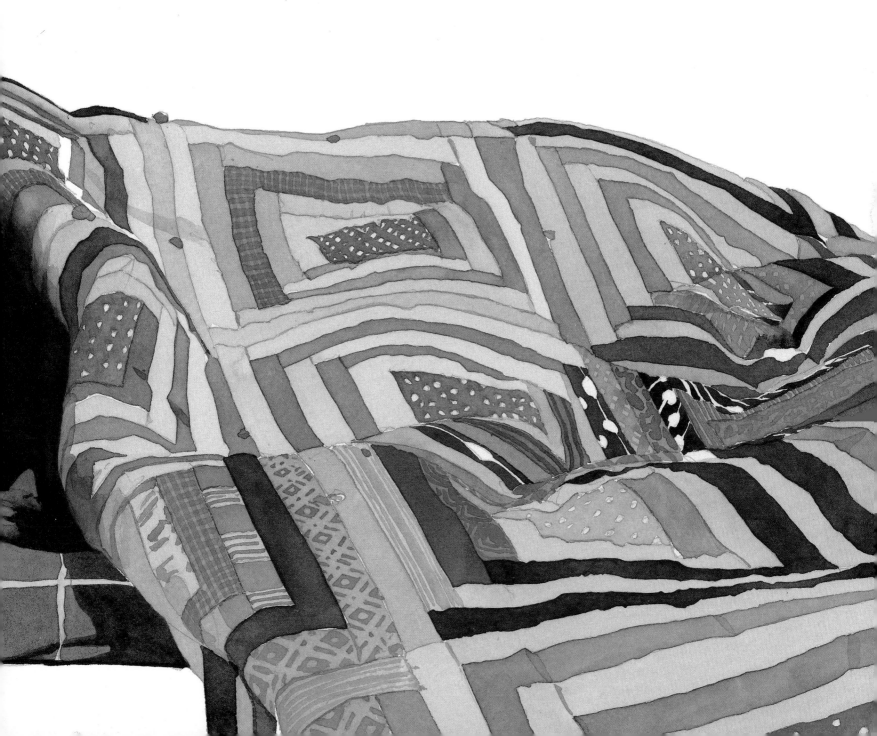

"I have to go back to work now," Grandpa says.
"Will you stay here with Rosie and take care of him for me?"

"Yes."